The Dragon's Tale
and Other Animal Fables of the Chinese Zodiac

Demi

HENRY HOLT AND COMPANY · NEW YORK

THE
RAT'S TALE

Once there was a rat who lived under a rock. He was sad
because his burrow was uncomfortable and finding food in the
hot sun was hard work. One day he looked up at the sky and said,
"How powerful the sun is! I wish I could be the sun, floating free above the
earth." In that moment, the rat became the sun. He cast his sizzling rays
toward the earth, beaming with pride. Soon a small cloud floated in front of him,
blocking his light. "I never thought a cloud could be stronger than the sun," he
thought. "How I wish I were a cloud." Suddenly the rat found he was a fluffy white
cloud. But before long, the wind blew him apart. "I never knew how powerful the
wind could be. I wish I were the wind," he cried. Instantly the rat became the wind,
blowing houses into the sea and ships onto the land. He rejoiced in his power—
until he hit a large rock. "Nothing could be stronger than a rock," he thought. "I
must be a rock!" He was turned into a rock, but soon he found that a rat had
burrowed underneath him. "How uncomfortable it is to be a rock!" he said
with a sigh. "I just wish I could be a rat again." His last wish was granted,
and from that day on, the rat never complained again.

To be at peace with oneself
is worth the sun, moon,
and stars together.

THE
OX'S TALE

Once upon a time some oxen were grazing in a field together, in peace and friendship. Several tigers lurked nearby, hoping the oxen would scatter so the tigers could make a juicy meal of them. As long as the oxen stayed together, the tigers knew they could not attack.

Then the tigers had an idea. They began to whisper evil stories and gossip of one ox against the other, which the birds heard. The birds flew to the oxen and landed on their backs. As the birds chattered away, repeating the tigers' evil stories and gossip, the oxen eyed each other with distrust. They began to quarrel. Some charged at one another, and others grazed apart from the rest.

Now the tigers knew they would be eating well. They licked their lips and pounced upon the scattered oxen, making an easy meal of them all.

The quarrels of friends
are the opportunities
of foes.

THE
TIGER'S TALE

While hunting one day, a tiger trapped a fox.

"You can't eat me," declared the fox. "The Heavenly Dragon has appointed me king of all the animals. If you eat me, you'll be disobeying the laws of Heaven."

The tiger laughed at the fox, and opened his mouth wide to eat him.

"Stop!" cried the fox. "Before you eat me, let me prove to you that I am the king. Follow me, and watch how the other animals run when they see me."

This seemed fair to the tiger. He followed the fox into a clearing where many animals were resting. Sure enough, when the animals saw the fox and the tiger, they dashed away.

"See?" said the fox. "Now leave my kingdom!" The tiger, not realizing that the animals were really afraid of him, not the fox, scurried away.

Small creatures must
live by their wits.

THE
RABBIT'S TALE

Once there was a family of rabbits who lived near a big
fruit tree. One day a large piece of fruit dropped off a branch,
making a sound like thunder. The terrified rabbits ran away as fast as
their legs could carry them. A fox asked, "Why are you running?"

"Because the sky is falling!" the rabbits replied, and so the fox followed them.

A few paces later, a monkey asked, "Why are you running?"

"The sky is falling!" the fox replied, and so the monkey ran too. Soon a deer, a pig, a
buffalo, a rhinoceros, an elephant, a bear, a leopard, and a tiger were all running from
the falling sky.

They approached a lion. "Why are you all running?" he roared.

"Because the sky is falling!" they cried.

"How do you know?" the lion asked.

The tiger said the leopard had told him, the leopard said the bear had told him, the
bear had been told by the elephant, who had been told by the rhinoceros, and so
on. The rabbits squeaked, "Come, we'll show you where the sky fell."

They led the lion to the fruit tree and said, "The sky fell here!" Just then,
another big piece of fruit fell from the tree. The lion laughed and roared,
"The sky has fallen again!"

If someone tells a falsehood,
one hundred will
repeat it as true.

THE
DRAGON'S TALE

Once upon a time there was a flood, and many small rivers flowed into one big river. The big river was so deep and wide that the fish who had lived in smaller rivers thought it must be the greatest body of water in the whole world. They swelled with pride as they swam along in their new home.

How surprised they were, then, when their river emptied into the sea. They had never seen such a vast body of water. There they met the ruler of the sea, the Dragon King. "Oh!" the fishes cried. "I guess we didn't live in the greatest body of water in the world after all."

The Dragon King replied, "No river is as large as the sea. Many rivers flow into it, but it is never full. Still, the sea is not proud. It knows it is only part of the greatness of the earth, and only a speck of dust compared to the vastness of the universe."

The more you know,
the more you know
there is to know.

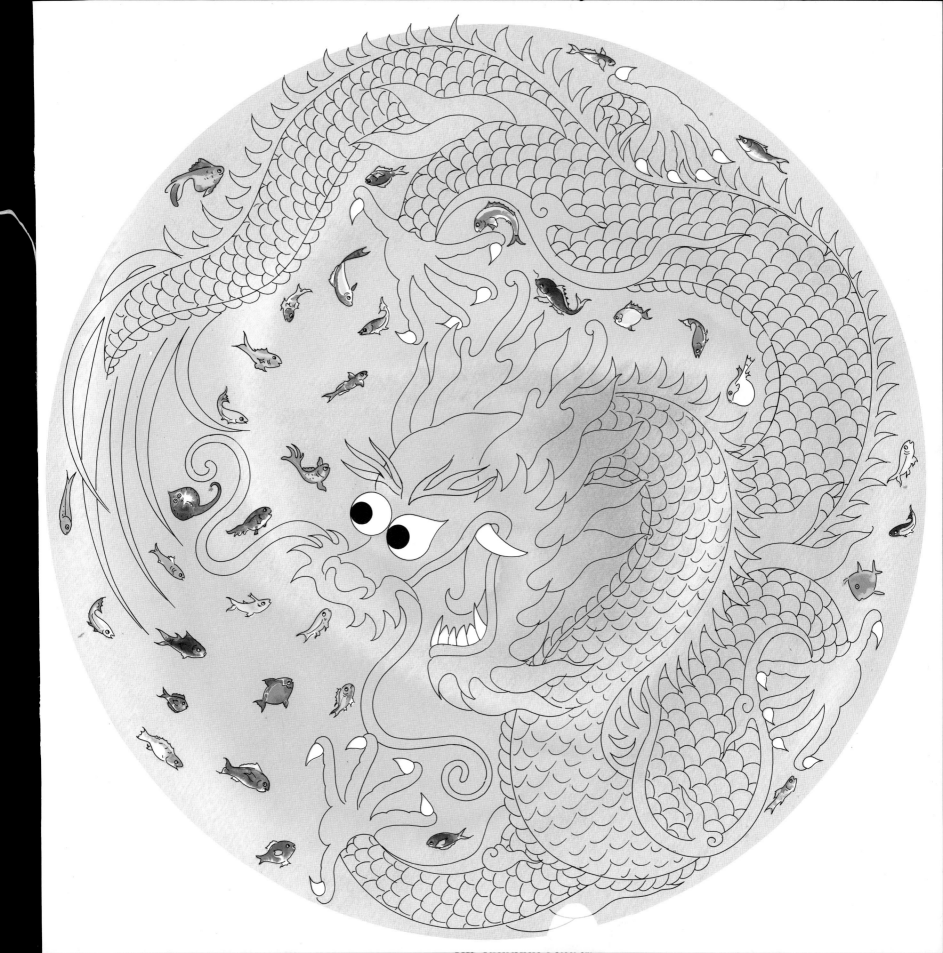

THE
SNAKE'S TALE

Once there were two snakes who lived in neighboring holes. One snake was called Spotted, the other, Striped.

One day Spotted was hungry. He hunted around his hole for an egg he had recently stolen, but couldn't find it anywhere. He left the hole and looked around, but saw only his neighbor, Striped. "Look how he slinks about so sneakily," thought Spotted. "And the way his tongue flickers greedily. See how his eyes shift back and forth! Striped must have stolen my egg." But before Spotted could accuse him, Striped slithered away.

Spotted returned to his hole, and soon found his egg hidden in a dark corner. Later, he saw Striped slithering, flicking his tongue, and shifting his eyes, acting just as he had before. But this time, nothing about Striped made Spotted think he'd stolen an egg.

Beware of judging
by appearances.

THE
HORSE'S TALE

Once upon a time a tiny fly was buzzing around a horse's head. He became tired of zooming this way and that, and landed on the tip of the horse's ear. With a loud buzzing, he preened himself, stretching and flapping his wings. After a minute or two, feeling rested and beautified, he prepared to fly away. But before he left, he begged the horse's pardon for having used his ear as a resting place. "You must be very glad to have me go now!" he said.

The horse looked puzzled. "Why, I didn't even know you were there."

We are often of greater importance
in our own eyes than in the
eyes of our neighbor.

THE
GOAT'S TALE

Once there was a frog who lived in a shallow well. When a goat passed by, the frog shouted, "Look how blessed I am down here! I can hop along the sides of my well when I want to, and I can rest in a crevice when I need to. I can wallow all day long with only my head above water if I feel like it, or I can lie in the soft mud at the bottom. And at night I can see two stars in the circle of sky at the top. I am lord and master of this well! Why don't you come down and see that my way of living is best?"

The goat looked down at the frog for a moment, but did not jump into the well. He said, "Frog, I have climbed the high mountains and seen the great sea. The sea is more than ten thousand miles across, and more than ten thousand feet deep. Your little well is of no consequence compared to the vastness of the sea. And what are your two stars compared to the billions in the universe? You no more understand the world than a mosquito could carry a mountain, or an ant swim in a river. Frog, you only see the world from the bottom of a well."

Those with a narrow view cannot
know the immensity
of the sky.

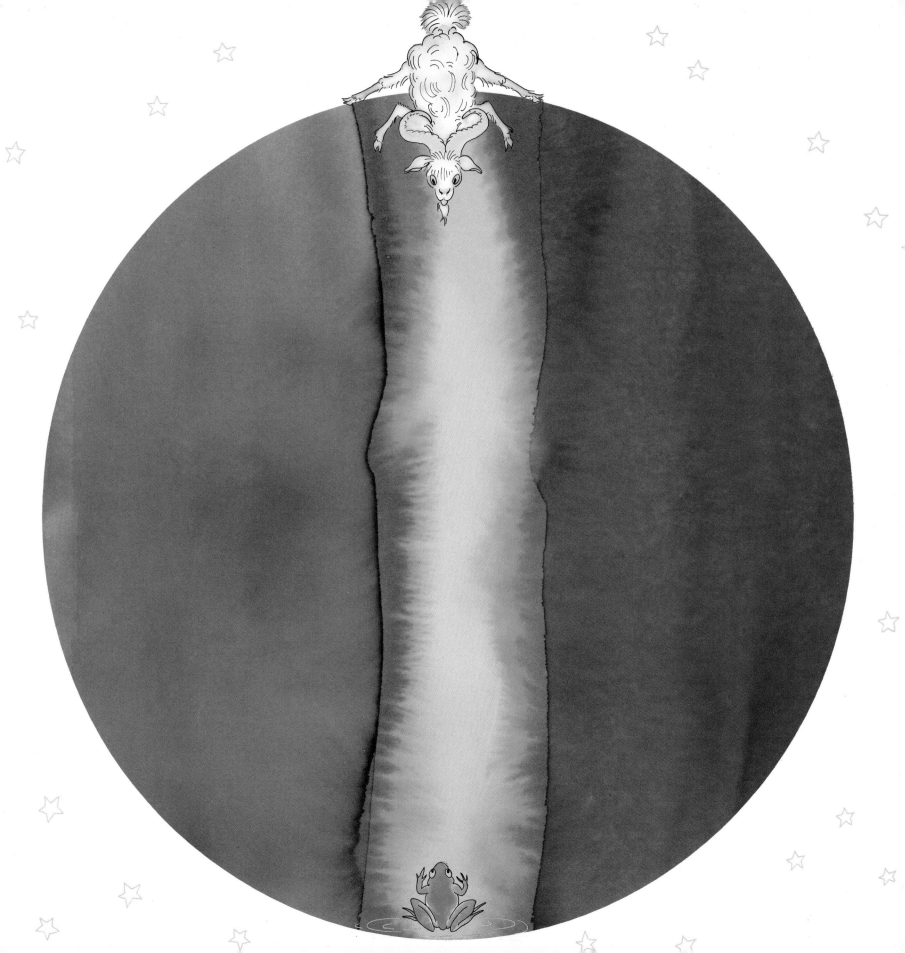

THE
MONKEY'S TALE

One evening some monkeys were playing by a well.
The smallest monkey leaned over the edge of the well and
looked in. There, at the bottom, was the round, bright moon!
"The moon has fallen into the well!" he shouted. All of the monkeys
gathered around the well and peered down. "We must fish it out at once!"
they cried. So they climbed a nearby tree and made a monkey chain down
into the well. The smallest monkey, at the end of the chain, reached for the
moon, but all he scooped up was a handful of water. The surface of the water
rippled, breaking the moon into pieces. "Oh, I've broken the moon," he said. The
other monkeys scolded him, but soon the water grew still, and the round, bright
moon appeared as it had before. Once again, the smallest monkey tried to grab the
moon, but once again he broke it.

By now the other monkeys in the chain were complaining that their arms and
tails hurt. Just then, the oldest monkey happened to look up, and saw the
moon hanging in the sky. He called to the others, "There's a new moon in
the sky! The old one must have been thrown into the well!" With that, all
the monkeys climbed out of the well and rejoiced at the sight of the
new moon.

Ignorance is bliss.

THE
ROOSTER'S TALE

Once there was a rooster who lived on a farm. Every morning, upon seeing the first rays of sunlight, he would throw back his head and let out a piercing "Cock-a-doodle-doo!" And every morning, the sun seemed to stop for a minute and look down at the rooster before rising into the sky.

One morning, the rooster hailed the sun and asked him why he always hesitated before rising. The sun replied, "I am the timekeeper for the planets. I must be exact. Therefore, I always wait for you to crow before I rise. Then I am sure it is morning." "But," said the rooster, "I crow only after seeing the first rays of the sun!"

The world is often made
up of the blind
leading the blind.

THE
DOG'S TALE

Once upon a time an old dog asked his pup, "Which is closer, the city or the sun?"

"The sun, of course!" replied the pup.

"And why do you say the sun?" asked the old dog.

"That's easy," answered the pup. "I can see the sun from here, but I can't see the city."

The old dog thought his pup was very clever, and took him to the city to show him off. When they reached the city, he told his son the names of all the animals who lived there.

The old dog gathered a crowd around the pup, and asked him again, "Now tell us, which is closer, the city or the sun?"

Quickly the pup replied, "The city, of course."

The old dog's mouth dropped in disappointment. "But—but only yesterday you told me the sun was closer!"

"Yes," said the pup. "But that was before I met all these animals from the city. Have you ever seen anyone who came from the sun?"

From the mouths of babes
comes great wisdom.

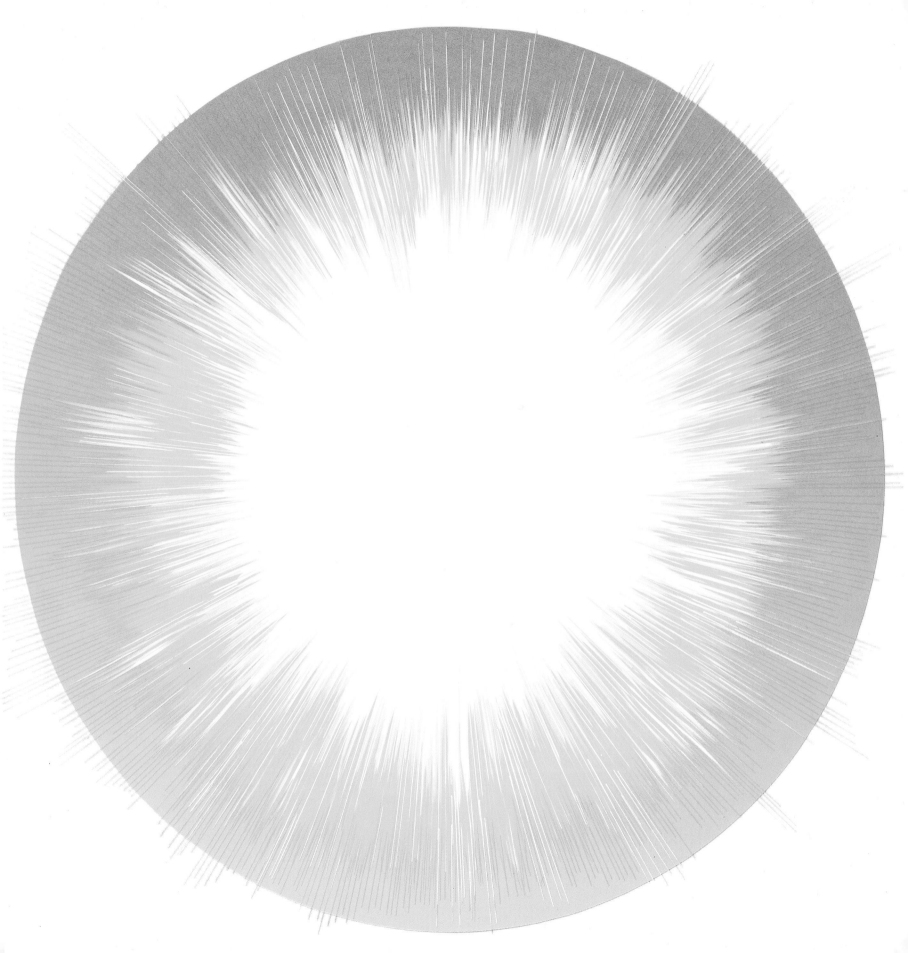

THE
BOAR'S TALE

Once there was a boar who thought he was the greatest and strongest animal in the universe. He pranced about trying to get the other animals to notice him. But no one did. This made the boar very angry, and he began charging about the forest, becoming angrier and angrier. While he snorted and ran, he smashed against a tree, which knocked one of his tusks crooked and gashed his side. This made him even angrier—so furious that he charged right into the tree itself! His tusks were stuck so deeply into the tree trunk that the boar was suspended in mid-air. How silly he felt when the gentle rabbits and birds had to pull him out by the tail!

Pride invites calamity;
humility reaps
its harvest.

Henry Holt and Company, Inc.
Publishers since 1866
115 West 18th Street
New York, New York 10011
Henry Holt is a registered
trademark of Henry Holt and Company, Inc.
Copyright © 1996 by Demi
Published in Canada by Fitzhenry & Whiteside Ltd.,
195 Allstate Parkway, Markham, Ontario L3R 4T8.

Library of Congress Cataloging-in-Publication Data. Demi. The dragon's tale and other animal fables of the Chinese
zodiac / retold and illustrated by Demi.   Summary: A collection of fables about the twelve animals of the
Chinese   zodiac. 1. Fables,   Chinese. 2. Tales–China. [1. Fables. 2. Folklore–China.] I. Title. PZ8.2.D3Dr
1996   398.2'0951–dc20   [E]   95-44932   ISBN 0-8050-3446-3 / First Edition—1996. Printed in the United States
of America on acid-free paper. ∞

1   3   5   7   9   10   8   6   4   2

Traditional paints were used: Black from ten parts pine soot; Blues and Greens from azurite, malachite, and indigo;
Reds from cinnabar, realgar, and orpiment; with Brilliant Red from a flowering vine; Umbar from iron oxide called
limonite; Yellow from the sap of the rattan plant; and White from lead or pulverized oyster shells. The colors were
then mixed with stag horn, fish, or ox glue, or glue made from the pulp of the soap bean. To all, powdered jade was
added for good fortune! The brushes were made of sheep, rabbit, goat, weasel, and wolf hairs picked in autumn for
pliancy. A brush of one mouse whisker was used for extremely delicate work. Changes were made by applying the
juice of the apricot seed.